END OF LINE

A COLLECTION OF SCIENCE FICTION SHORT STORIES

J. R. FRONTERA

Published by
TIN CAN

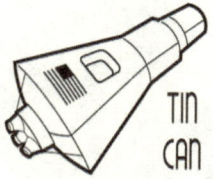

An imprint of Wordwraith Books, LLC
705-B SE Melody Lane #147
Lee's Summit, MO 64063
http://www.wordwraiths.com

Version 2.0

http://www.jrfrontera.com

Cover art by Get Covers
Formatting by Charity Chimni

BOOKS BY J. R. FRONTERA

All books available on Amazon.com and most other online retailers, wherever books are sold.

THE LEGACY OF LUCKY LOGAN

(scifi western)

Bargain at Bravebank

Bastard of Blessing

Bones in Blackbird

Demon at Devil's Deep

(and more coming soon)

N'SPACE

(humorous space opera)

Galapalooza

The Starburst Inn

(and more coming soon)

STARSHIP ASS

(humorous space opera)

Of Sporks, Overlords, and Moon Worms

Of Donkeys, Gods, and Space Pirates

Of Donkeys, Dogs, and Rogue Bits

Of Donkeys, Cogs, and Hot Bodies

COMPLETE

For a fully updated book list check out https://jrfrontera.com.

WORDWRAITH BOOKS

PRESENTS

END OF LINE

A COLLECTION OF SCIENCE
FICTION SHORT STORIES

WRITTEN BY

J. R. FRONTERA

BLACK-MARKET BODY

Richard Montgomery smoothed his linen shirt and watched from behind the one-way mirrored glass as three guards escorted Dimitrii Lagunov into the Recipient room. The prisoner wore the usual neon-orange jumpsuit, but beneath that, the skin was wonderfully free of tattoos. And beneath that, the organs were remarkably healthy for a thirty-five-year-old male of Dimitrii's profession.

Mother was right. The small towns have all the good ones.

The big cities might have had wider selections, but the wait lists were long and the clean Recipients were always in high demand. He would have never been able to secure a body like Dimitrii's on such short notice anywhere else but here, in the middle of nowhere in the middle of the Midwest.

Dimitrii's wrists and ankles were cuffed and linked to the thick leather belt around his waist with a short, heavy chain, and Richard frowned.

The drawback of Transferring into a prisoner was, of course, waking up in those chains. And that terrible orange jumpsuit. He'd never liked the fact these procedures were done on prison property, even if it was supposedly more secure than the alternative of taking prisoners off-site.

The Transfer nurse gave him a sympathetic smile. She was young and beautiful, and likely had no idea what it was like to be waiting to change bodies.

"Is this your first Transference?" she asked.

Richard shrugged and fidgeted. "Yeah," he said. "Why?" A wave of anxiety swelled as the convict on the other side of the

1

glass sat down in the treatment chair without protest or struggle.

Didn't he know what was about to happen?

She shook her head and tucked a strand of hair behind her ear. "You look a little nervous. That guy is pretty scary, though, huh?"

Richard scoffed. "He's a vile human being."

The nurse blinked. "But you chose him for your Transfer..."

Richard looked at her and lifted an eyebrow.

"Of course. He deserves to die, I deserve to live. I'll be using his body, that's all."

She nodded, and another smile flitted across her face. "Of course. Well, as far as bodies go, he's a looker. If, you know, you get rid of the whole serial killer mentality."

"Which I will." Richard turned his attention back to Dimitrii and ignored the cold slither of doubt in his chest. *I will. He may be a murderer, but a man used to killing is no match for a man used to dying.* He swallowed hard and cleared his throat, then straightened his shoulders. "You know, it'd be a lot easier on everyone if they'd legalize the use of Transfer volunteers already."

"Oh, I know. I heard the bill is being put to a vote in the House this month."

Richard blew a breath through his teeth.

Well, maybe it'd officially be legalized by his *next* Transference.

"You don't think legalizing Transfer volunteers would ever lead to a Transfer Draft of just *anyone*, do you, sir?" She tried to sound casual, but the strain in her voice made it clear she thought it might be a real concern.

"Preposterous!" He turned away from her and hobbled

back and forth in front of the one-way window, his polished mahogany cane making muffled rubberized squeaks against the smooth white linoleum. "Unfounded fears of idiotic radicals! Meant to send the rest of us into panic and prevent any real progress on the methods of Transference!"

The nurse dropped her eyes away at his outburst, but he wasn't done yet.

"With or without volunteers, there will always be criminals waiting on death row with bodies that shouldn't be wasted. Transfers are already limited to the availability of Recipients ... using volunteers would open up Transference as an option for more people. That's all." He pivoted on his heel and pointed a finger in her direction. "And that's what those extremists are really afraid of. Transference itself. They want it all shut down!"

Too dangerous, they said. Too many opportunities for things to go wrong. *Unfounded fears of idiotic radicals!* There had been thousands and thousands of successful Transfers over the last few decades. They had the process down to an art....

The nurse gave an uneasy chuckle. "That will never happen. For sure."

"Most certainly not." Richard went back to pacing. He focused on the various aches and pains in his joints, the stiffness in his hands and hips, instead of the unease rolling around in his gut.

Do you want to live the rest of your days like this? No you do not! Shape up and get yourself together! That body over there is in peak physical condition, and it's just for you. All you have to do is take it.

He hadn't suffered through months of those ridiculous pre-Transfer counseling sessions, meditation exercises, and rigorous psychological testing to get cold feet now at the very end. Hell no.

He'd paid for this, signed the contract, promised Mother. And he would do it.

"Mr. Montgomery?"

The nurse's soft voice caught his attention.

He turned to see her at the side of his own treatment chair, a mirror image of Mr. Lagunov's, leather restraints and all ... in case the Transfer did not go according to plan. She held out a hand toward it in invitation, as if it were a luxurious feather bed instead of some type of operating-table-dental-chair-hybrid.

His instant of hesitation was masked by his outwardly confident, yet stunted strides forward.

If anything, he'd be glad when this was over and he could walk unassisted again. The nurse took his cane as he settled himself onto the edge of the chair, then helped him ease back into a semi-reclining position. She buckled the padded restraints around his wrists and ankles with care.

Dr. Rocha swept into the room as if on cue, a formidably tall woman with brown hair beginning to turn silver and eyes the color of a stormy sea.

Dr. Rocha had undergone Transference five times herself, a large part of why Richard had personally selected her.

"Good afternoon, Mr. Montgomery!" Dr. Rocha flashed him a smile as white as the walls.

"Ready to get underway, are we?"

Richard nodded, and the bare remains of his own mouse-gray hair scratched against the chair's headrest. He rubbed his fingertips together and felt callouses there, formed from years of sailing and loading antique guns. Funny how he'd never really noticed them before.

The pre-Transference counselors had said such sudden self-reflection was normal when a person faced leaving the only body they had ever known. But Richard had no use for it. It tasted too much like uncertainty, and that was something he had never entertained. He'd known he was eligible for Transference for greater than fifty years now, plenty of time to get used to the idea. And he'd had his own genetic Original for even longer: a full, rich seventy-six years. It was time to move on.

"Been waiting too long, Doc," he said. "Let's get this done."

"Very good, very good." She checked his vitals and bustled around the bank of equipment on the other side of the room.

The assisting nurse applied electrodes to Richard's temples, and the faint scent of apples wafted from her hair. He winced as she tucked a needle into his vein for the IV drip.

"The anesthesia will take effect shortly," Dr. Rocha said, typing something on her tablet. "You'll go into a deep sleep. Just remember your exercises ... the first Transference can be rather disorienting.

We don't want you to get lost now, do we?" She chuckled, but Richard did not share her humor.

If he got lost in there, he wouldn't be coming back. In any form. And that was no laughing matter. He chose not to reply, instead turning his head to look through the one-way window one last time.

Dimitrii Lagunov stared right at him.

Richard walked forward without a cane, his pin-striped

suit impeccably pressed. Obsidian cuff links shimmered in the light, exact matches to the large obsidian stone set in gold on his left ring finger. A part of his mind questioned the ring—after all, he had never married.

But then he remembered the pre-Transfer counseling sessions. It was common for the subconscious to conjure up everything a person had wanted to be and everything they had wished to have during the Transference process. It was the brain's way of fighting the change, the experts said, of clinging desperately to its original identity.

The Ego, as it were, making its egotistical stand.

I'd hardly say I ever wished to be married. More trouble than it's worth, surely.

He walked onward, through stark whiteness.

The coaching sessions made a lot more sense from this side of the Transference. They'd told him to keep walking forward, no matter what, and now he understood. There was no sound, no sensation of movement, no way to tell if he was making any actual progress.

This is pointless. Why keep walking if I'm not going anywhere?

For an instant, his steps slowed, but then he resumed the steady pace. If all those counselors didn't know what they were talking about, why had he paid them so much money?

Just do what they said to do and get this over with.

He went through the motions. One foot in front of the other, arms swinging, head held high, and hoped it would be enough.

A wall loomed in front of him abruptly and forced him to stop. Richard frowned up at it. That was something no one had mentioned. No one had ever said anything about a wall.

He looked to his left, then to his right, but it appeared to be a never-ending expanse of flat gray cinder-block. Bewilderment scratched at his consciousness. What did he do now? A person couldn't very well walk forward with a wall in front of him, could he? Or *could* he? It *was* a dream-world, and maybe that was the point of walking forward no matter what.

Richard took a cautious step forward and brought himself right up against the wall, but it felt quite solid. The toes of his polished Oxfords scuffed against its base, and the rough texture of the bricks pressed into his palms as he leaned into it and pushed. No use. This dream wall was as solid as any in the real world.

He stepped back and sighed. Looks like the counselors were full of shit. Bastards. When I wake up, I'm calling my lawyer.

He turned right and followed the wall until he came to an opening. Relief washed over him, only to curdle into dread as he walked through it and recognized what he'd stepped into: a maze.

A maze of gray cinder-block walls. No one had ever said anything about a damn maze, either, and Dr. Rocha's comment about getting lost now seemed even less amusing. He scowled and shook his head, but there was little choice other than to keep moving.

Oh yes, when I get out of here I'm going to give those counselors an earful! Dr. Rocha, too. She should have known it'd be like this. She could have said something, given me some kind of warning! This is absolutely unacceptable!

He threaded his way through the narrow corridors, and hours passed ... or maybe only minutes. He had nothing to mark the time or help him remember where he had already been. The cinder-blocks were as unremarkable as the blank white sky, every one exactly the same, the mortar between them perfectly smoothed. He found dead ends and turned around, found dead ends and turned around, found dead ends and turned around.…

How am I ever supposed to find anything or anybody in here? He stopped walking and cursed profusely.

"I did not know a man of your upbringing could swear so effectively," said a voice in a rich Russian accent.

Richard spun around. The walls behind him were gone, and a man sitting on a large black recliner had appeared in their place. Richard stiffened and squinted at his new companion. The man's black hair had been smoothed back, his dark eyes reflecting the black of his shiny shoes, pressed pants, and button-up shirt. He casually crossed one ankle over the opposite knee and tapped at his lips with one finger.

Recognition registered at last in Richard's dream-brain. *Dimitrii Lagunov!* Without the orange jumpsuit and chains, the man cleaned up well. Richard smirked and crossed his arms. *Well done, Richard. Very good choice, indeed. A body to match the brains at last.* He cleared his throat.

"Mr. Lagunov. Good to finally meet you in person. Sort of. Although I must admit, no one told me to expect you."

Dimitrii smiled, revealing remarkably straight teeth. "No, for certain, they would not have told you that." He stood from his plush recliner and walked to a suddenly appeared sideboard. "Would you like a drink?"

Richard arched an eyebrow. "Well, sure."

They never said I couldn't have a drink here.

"Your favorite, or mine?"

Richard frowned. "I don't think I understand—"

Dimitrii hissed something in Russian and shook his head. "Kat is right. They tell you nothing out there."

"Who doesn't tell me what?" Richard shifted on his feet as

the rest of the maze melted away and left more empty white-ness in its wake.

Was it supposed to be like this? They had never said, exactly...

Dimitrii pushed a tumbler of whiskey—Richard's favorite —into his hand.

"The doctors," Dimitrii said. "The counselors. All fools." The man went back to his recliner and sat down, swirling his own drink before taking a sip. "Nobody remembers what happens during Transference once they wake up on other side, and this is problem."

Richard shook his head as he processed the words through the thick accent. "That's not true. The post-Transfer identity questions—"

"That is subconscious." Dimitrii gave a dismissive grunt. "Otherwise, why so many mental exercises before Transfer? They train your subconscious self, not your conscious self."

Unease drifted through Richard's stomach, but outwardly he only scoffed. "Dr. Rocha said—"

"Dr. Rocha." Dimitrii chuckled and sipped again. "She lied, also. The more you Transfer, the more you remember, yes, but only in pieces like ... what is your word ... déjà vu? Yes, like déjà vu. And only in dreams. Such memories are not truth, cannot be foundation for Transfer education, yet that is what they do."

Richard scowled. But then, wasn't he here to replace Dimitrii's consciousness? And everyone knew the displaced consciousness often did not give up without a fight. This whole conversation was merely Dimitrii Lagunov's last ditch attempt at survival. The initial flutter of panic eased, and Richard sipped at his drink, smiling as the smoky warmth slid down his throat. "And how would you know anything about it?" he asked.

Dimitrii smiled as well. "Because I have been through it before, Mr. Montgomery. Many times. Sometimes I remember what happened. We are dreaming now, yes? This is when I remember best." He winked.

Richard was in mid-sip of whiskey, but as he took in Dimitrii's words, the flavor soured. He choked down the alcohol and attempted to smother a cough. "Impossible. I checked into your background, your medical records especially. Something like that would have shown up."

Dimitrii full-out laughed, his amber tones as rich as the whiskey. "They *try* to track it, yes. They *try* to have regulations, to have records. But Mr. Montgomery, please. We speak of *consciousnesses*. Everything we are, all experience and interpretation, all here in collection of chemicals and electricity." He tapped at his temple, black eyes shining. "Separate that from physical, and what is it? A ghost. Invisible. Impossible to track, impossible to measure. We exist in wires now, Mr. Montgomery ... wires connected to many other wires and other machines, hundreds of other possibilities. How many times did *both* consciousnesses go into oblivion, you think? Did they tell you odds?"

Richard swallowed hard and wrestled down the anger that rose hot to his face. They had told him the odds of a successful operation, sure ... but no one had said anything about *both* consciousnesses being lost. *Lawyer. I need my lawyer. None of this is right. Someone is getting sued for malpractice!* "Of course they did," he blustered. He wouldn't give Dimitrii the pleasure of being right.

"All false. You cannot create odds without all numbers.

And I guarantee they do not have all numbers. Listen, you think those fools are only ones with this technology?"

Just what in the hell is that supposed to mean?

Richard looked around again, though he wasn't entirely sure what he hoped to see. He found only the stretching expanse of white, Dimitrii's armchair, the criminal, and himself. Even the sideboard had vanished. The only evidence it had ever existed in the first place was the glass of whiskey in his hand and the glass of vodka in Dimitrii's. *What's taking so long? Shouldn't this Transfer be over already?*

He turned back to Dimitrii and cleared his throat.

Keep him talking. Distract him. "Are you saying you Transferred illegally?"

Dimitrii nodded once. "Now you are beginning to follow. Think I killed those people in fun?"

He clicked his tongue against the roof of his mouth and shook his head. "No. They had purpose. Black market for Transfer bodies pays very well, Mr. Montgomery."

Richard frowned. Unease crept back into his veins as he met Dimitrii's flat stare. "But ... you can't Transfer into a dead body..."

Dimitrii stood and Richard startled as the sideboard obediently appeared once more.

The man refilled his glass, the tinkle of ice against the tumbler's sides echoing in the emptiness around them. "Not so. It is easier with dead body—there is no native consciousness to fight. You have to be smart, though, not damage body too much, and Transfer quick." His expression turned thoughtful for a moment, and his brow furrowed.

"Even so, it does not always work." He grunted, then turned to face Richard and leaned forward as if sharing a vital secret. "The bodies police say I murdered were failures," he whispered loudly, then shrugged. "The rest I took are still alive, happy, only now with different people in their skulls."

Richard found his mouth open and shut it with a click. Sweat dampened the silk shirt beneath his suit, and he shifted his shoulders uncomfortably.

He didn't remember ever sweating in a dream.

Dimitrii leaned back against the bar. "Bureau of Consciousness Replacement does not want public to know they can Transfer to dead people. If everyone knows, there might be more people like me." He snorted, apparently amused by that idea.

"And dead people are easy to take care of, anyway. Simply incinerate them, and they are gone. BCR want everyone to believe there is no need for using dead bodies." He grinned. "But criminals," he waved his hand in a grand gesture to indicate himself, "criminals are ... what you call, a pain in ass. Expensive. Taking up room and resources. And if one is bad enough to deserve death ... why waste perfectly good body, no?"

Richard cleared his throat, then forced himself to raise his glass in a mock toast. "That's right." He took a large gulp, his gaze never leaving Dimitrii. Nothing about this felt right. Shouldn't he have woken up by now? Shouldn't something be changing, at least? *What is going on? Why haven't they aborted the Transfer? If Dr. Rocha isn't going to stop this, then I will!* "Thank you for the stimulating conversation," he said abruptly, setting his glass down on the sideboard. "But it's time to get on with this."

Dimitrii gave another shrug and sipped at his refilled glass. "Yes, I suppose it is your time."

Something in the man's tone stopped Richard mid-step as

he was about to leave. He twisted to look over his shoulder. "Excuse me?"

Dimitrii pointed upward and made small circles in the air with his index finger. "I watch you looking 'round here, nervous as cornered little mouse. You know something is wrong."

Richard squared his shoulders, smoothing the front of his jacket. "Nonsense." A sliver of panic clutched at his chest and made his voice shake, but he ignored it. *He's baiting you. Trying to intimidate you. Don't let him get to you!* "There's nothing wrong at all. I just wasn't expecting to be delayed by the likes of you." He spun on his heel and marched off.

"Perhaps not," Dimitrii called out behind him. "But you *did* expect more."

The statement made Richard stop again, and he turned around despite himself. "So?" he demanded, tired of these games. "What does that matter? A man in your position should know better than most that expectations don't always measure up to reality."

"That is so," Dimitrii said.

The easy acknowledgement made Richard's gut churn.

"But do you think this talk was for my health?" The man scoffed. "It is important you stay here certain length of time. If you were someone else, I would have let you rot in that maze. I made exception for you, a man of great influence. Our talk was more interesting way to wait, yes?"

Richard squinted at the man, dread racing along his nerves like a razor. "And what were we waiting for, exactly?"

The criminal looked around again before his gaze came back to hold Richard's stare. "This should be Ego's stand," the man said, walking slowly toward him. "It should be paradise, your dream-world. But instead ... nothing. Nothing but you and I. Why, Mr. Montgomery? Why do we see nothing?"

Richard gaped for a moment. His pulse pounded in his temples as he struggled for some kind of response. But then the rage leapt up, dampening the uncertainty and fear. *I don't have to answer to the likes of a murderer like him!*

"Because you are in coma, Richard," the man whispered, his voice still somehow as loud and pervasive as thunder. "That is what we waited for."

A smile grew across his face, and his eyes gleamed as he advanced now with alarming speed. "Makes it almost as easy as if you were dead."

Dr. Katerina Rocha handed her identification to the guard, then leaned over to hold her eye in front of the retina scanner. It beeped a confirmation, but the prison personnel knew her well and, as such, paid little attention to the machine's judgment. This whole process was more of a formality at this point, Katerina being one of the most widely known Certified Consciousness Replacement Physicians in the country. But they went through it every time, anyway.

She clipped her ID back to the pocket of her lab coat as the lock on the reinforced door in front of her disengaged with a heavy thump. A buzzer sounded, and she reached out to pull the door open, gaining access to the Recipient room beyond at last. Miss Sorenson, her assisting nurse, had stayed behind in the Donor room to clean up. No matter how this

Transfer had ended, neither Mr. Richard Montgomery nor Mr. Dimitrii Lagunov would be returning to that body.

Besides, sometimes this part could end badly, and she preferred to keep the nurses out of it. *Especially for this one.*

The body of Dimitrii Lagunov stirred in his restraints as Katerina drew up to the side of the reclining treatment chair. She nodded to the three guards, who still stood on high alert. As the man on the chair shifted and groaned, she brought up the tablet from under her arm, took a deep breath, and began running down the list of post-Transfer identity-confirmation questions. "Try to relax, sir. Do you know who you are?"

"I—I think so ... yes. Yes. I'm ... Richard Montgomery. The Third."

She paused, mentally analyzing his speech patterns, trying to determine if they had changed at all. So far, too subtle to tell. Further conversation would make any variation more apparent. "Your middle name?"

The man winced, his voice gruff. "Manley. Never liked that one."

"Your father's name?"

Richard's new face shot her a glare. "Richard Montgomery the Second. Obviously."

She paused again and tried to ignore the impatience clawing at her heart. *Easy. Take it slow. Don't rush it.* "Your mother's full maiden name and date of birth?"

"Hannah MaryAnn Ott, born March 17th, 2245."

"Your BPM identification number?"

The man sighed heavily and rolled his eyes.

"XA89MP4509CV7610HI5."

Katerina double-checked each letter and number before she nodded in approval and marked a check next to the box on her tablet. "And last but not least, I need your Individual Transfer Code, please."

Richard squirmed briefly in his restraints, and she held her breath. "That would be ... Gamma. Five. Cedar. Fork. And blue mailbox."

She exhaled slowly, silently, and checked off each word, the fluttering anxiety in the pit of her stomach perfectly masked behind an enthusiastic smile. She glanced at the guards. "Excellent! Looks like we have another successful full Transfer!"

They relaxed somewhat then, giving up their stiff postures to begin the finalization procedure.

She turned her attention back to the man on the chair, and her voice carried only the slightest tremble of anticipation. "Congratulations, Mr. Montgomery, and welcome to your healthier, younger self!"

Richard returned the smile, then glanced down to his new body and flexed his hands into fists as the guards unlocked the restraints. "Thanks, Doc. It will take some getting used to."

Katerina reached down to help him sit, her skin lighting up with fire wherever they touched.

So many years since they'd last had physical contact.... She swallowed hard and patted him on the shoulder, fighting to keep her focus. "It always does," she managed to say. "But it won't be as bad as you think. The public re-identification process is worse, to tell the truth." She forced a chuckle.

"It's a necessary evil, but I'm sure you'll do fine."

She brought up her tablet once more, then signed and q-fired the post-Transfer orders to the Re-identification Wing of Saint John's Hospital. "The guards will process your release and show you out," she said. "I'll meet you at my car, and then we'll head over to the hospital for your post-Transfer tests and get the ball rolling on updating your identification records. It'll take a few hours, but we should have everything all squared away by this evening."

Richard nodded wordlessly. He tried to wet dry lips and rubbed absently at his throat with one hand as the guards moved around behind him, shutting down the equipment.

"Thirsty?" she asked casually. Severe thirst was a common side-effect of the Transfer. It was also part of their pre-arranged signal. Her heart thundered in her ears. *Don't get your hopes up too high. There's still the possibility of lingering consciousness overlap...*

"Very."

"Of course, Mr. Montgomery. Of course. What'll it be? I'll have water for you at the car, and they'll probably give you an IV at the hospital. Usually do, to be safe." *I'm talking too much, and too quickly. Pull it together, Kat.*

Time seemed to freeze as Richard glanced up at her, only halfway sheepish. "Anything stronger, by chance? Vodka, perhaps?"

Kat's fingers reactively tightened around the edge of her tablet. Relief exploded through her chest, flooding warmth all the way down to her toes. Their eyes locked for the briefest of moments, and in those dark depths, she saw a familiar gleam. Her smile widened into a grin as she gave a slow nod. "I'm not sure that's such a good idea so soon after your Transference, Mr. Montgomery. But I'll see what I can do. Now ... let's get you out of here."

__Author's Note:__ This short story idea was originally conceived as a novel, and will likely someday be seen in that capacity. But in the meantime, I was trying to practice more short story form, so I wrote a story that would illustrate the novel's basic premise and also set up the main villain. This was that story.

GRAY

The sky was gray the day they put my father in the ground, and for once I missed the sun.

Shoulders hunched against the biting breeze, I jammed my hands into my pockets and curled my fingers into fists. Had it always been so cold here?

I didn't remember. But then, I didn't remember the grass ever looking so mangled and dead, the sky looking so bleak, the faces of those still allowed to live on Earth looking so pale. I watched them all from a distance, standing half-concealed behind the twisted, gnarled trunk of a giant oak. Its bare branches shivered in the winter wind, spread out high over my head.

I watched the sparse group of family standing next to Father's hole in the ground, dressed in black. They dabbed at their eyes and noses with finely embroidered handkerchiefs.

I didn't recognize any of them. Didn't know any of them. I wondered if Father ever told them what had really happened to me, or if he'd written me off completely the day I stormed out of the barn in a teenage rage. I wondered if that had effectively erased my existence from family history. For a son to deny a role in the family business held for generations, to deny the birth-given right to remain on the planet of humanity's origin ... in Father's eyes, there was no greater sin.

He never spoke to me again. Not even the day I'd showed up on his doorstep to tell him I was still alive, I had made it, and there was more to this galaxy than his little patch of Terran dirt.

He'd slammed the door in my face.

Not even the day he'd discovered what I actually did for a living, that my job was steeped in blood and lies and political maneuverings ... that I had killed.

Killed so many.

His face was stone that day, no hint of the twinkle in the blue eyes I'd seen so often as a child playing in his corn fields. Not a twitch of that hard, stern mouth that hadn't really smiled since Mother had died in that shuttle crash on my thirteenth birthday. He'd simply looked at me, stock-still and rigid, the only witness to what I had just done. The only witness I had ever allowed to live in my fifteen-year career.

Then he'd turned and walked away.

I don't know why I didn't go after him.

Sometimes I think part of me wanted him to know, *needed* him to know.

To see his reaction.

To see if he ... cared.

I broke the rules of my profession, the oath of my guild, and let him walk.

The authorities never came for me. Father knew, and he'd never told. Was that the extent of his love for his eldest son, then? Saving me from the gallows? Or was it the opposite, in fact ... not saving me from death, but condemning me to life?

One of the women next to the grave now clutched the mittened hands of two small children, a girl and a boy, maybe around eight and six. How sadly ironic I could know the intimate details of so many people's lives, memorize so much about a target I could fool anyone into thinking they were my own flesh and blood, my own best friend, but in reality my family—the people who should have been closest to me— were the real strangers. Were those children my cousins? A niece and nephew perhaps? A brother and sister, even?

I swallowed hard and blinked rapidly as the wind beat against my face. Tears leaked through my lashes and burned my skin like acid in the frigid air.

None of this mattered. It was over. Mother had gone long ago, and now Father too. There was nothing left for me here. I would never have to come back, never have to see the Earth-dwellers happy and safe on their generational farms, wallowing in their glorious amount of space and blissfully ignorant of everything happening in the skies above them.

I looked resentfully into the clouded heavens.

Rarely had I seen the sun in any extent aside from a fiery ball in passing beyond a spaceship window, or as some obscure object residing far outside the porthole of some dingy station. I hadn't felt the golden kiss of its warmth since ... since the day my father had been my only witness all those years ago.

It wouldn't come out for me now, I knew. Not after what I had done.

The sun had always loved my Father, and his farm.

I sighed heavily, breath clouding around my head to join its gray counterparts above. I gave one final glance to the unknown relatives surrounding the raw earth of my Father's grave, then spun on my heel and made my way back toward the rented transport. The ground was damp and spongy; everything washed in the miserable tint of death and sadness, as if by entering the ground my Father had made the entire planet aware of my deeds.

But it didn't matter anymore. I had broken the rules once, only once, and taken years to come full circle back to that mistake. In my profession you couldn't afford to make mistakes or break the rules. Not even once. It didn't matter that my Father had never told. I had built a reputation now, a reputation that ensured my survival. I could no longer afford a loose end, or the hope of someone coming to stop me.

It was too late now. I could never go back.

I stopped next to my transport and looked over my shoulder, breath rasping harshly through my teeth. The woman with the two children threw the first ceremonial shovel of dirt over Father's coffin as the mournful drone of a prayer echoed across the flat of the cemetery. My jaw clenched.

I only wished he would have *said* something to me, there before the end. Something, *anything*, just one last time. Just one word, some kind of acknowledgement—*any* kind of acknowledgment.

A nod, a frown, a shout, a cry. Any kind of surprise or condemnation. Even a damnation the likes of which he'd shouted at my back that last day I'd ever heard his voice would have been greatly welcome.

But he'd said nothing. Nothing at all. Just stared me right in the eyes with that stone-cold look, even as I'd slipped my blade smoothly between his ribs and up into his heart.

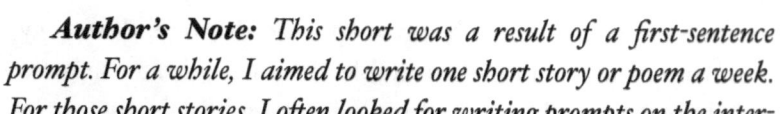

Author's Note: *This short was a result of a first-sentence prompt. For a while, I aimed to write one short story or poem a week. For those short stories, I often looked for writing prompts on the internet. The first sentence of this story was one such prompt. From that one sentence, this tale emerged.*

It ended up being an exploration of backstory for one of the characters in my upcoming space opera thriller novel, working title of Guardian Angel. *And it got pretty dark. The feel of the first sentence was so bleak and depressing from the start, that mood really took over the whole story. As to whether or not this character will ever find redemption ... that will have to wait for the novel. This one made it to the Second Read list at two SFWA-approved markets before ultimately still being rejected, and so here it lies for public consumption at last.*

IN COMPENSATION

She'd won! She'd actually won!

Maisy's hands flew to cover her mouth and muffle the shriek of excitement. She blinked away tears of exhilaration, but couldn't stop herself from bouncing on the balls of her feet.

The man and woman who'd brought her this wonderful news waited patiently on her porch, hands clasped neatly in front of them, small little smiles on their lips.

The woman was the first to speak. "The shuttle will arrive to pick you up tomorrow morning, 0800 sharp. Please be ready to go promptly. Space travel is not cheap, as I'm sure you know. The inter-solar ships won't be delayed for the sake of one passenger."

The man nodded in agreement. "This is a once-in-a-life-time opportunity, Miss Gallagher. Don't let it go to waste."

"Oh, I won't!" Maisy reached out and caught the woman's wrist, then wrung her hand in a hearty shake. "Thank you! Thank you so much!"

The woman's smile stretched, and she gently pulled her hand from Maisy's grip. "You are very welcome, Miss Gallagher. We'll leave you to get ready now. Twenty-four hours is not a lot of time to prepare for such a trip."

They turned and left with Maisy still thanking them, and she didn't stop until they'd clambered into their own shuttle and flown away. Not until then did she finally shut the door, feeling light as air. She practically skipped down the hall to her room, wanting to begin packing immediately.

She'd never been to the moon before, and they were right: twenty-four hours was not a lot of time to prepare!

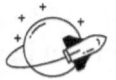

Three days later, she stood on the threshold of a moon farm. She craned her neck back to look up through the transparent bio-dome at the stretch of space and its infinite stars, the perfect sphere of Earth a gorgeous blue marble against the black, and mused over the strangeness of the contest that had brought her here.

An all-expenses-paid vacation to the moon, winnable by a simple essay on why she wanted to go to the moon, and how she might contribute to the mining efforts there during her stay. She'd always been good at essays, all her teachers had said so. *And yet I never thought an essay could land me on the moon!*

Her thoughts went to her mother as this farm's owners, Mildred and Alfred Honeyberry—a lovely elderly couple originally from Ohio—ushered her from the dome with its spectacular views into the close confines of the farmhouse itself. Her mother had begged her not to enter the contest, insisting that space travel was dangerous, and asking over and over again what could possibly be so great about the moon, anyway?

The view! Maisy smiled and followed along as her hosts went on with the droning tour of their modest abode.

Built of large, flexible plastic tubes filled with moon-dust and coiled into habitable structures, the farm's buildings really more resembled huge, alien bee hives in varying shades of gray instead of a functional hub of mining activity. But she wasn't going to tell her gracious hosts that. They seemed thrilled to have a guest, and when Mildred finally showed

Maisy to her room and left her to get settled, Maisy found a very expensive bottle of wine on her nightstand.

She picked it up in awe and turned the bottle over in her hands. Her mouth watered in anticipation. This was a bottle people on Earth could seldom afford to enjoy, much less those on the moon!

A small square of paper had been attached to the bottle's neck with black ribbon. She flipped it over to read the hand-written note:

"In compensation.

Sincerely,

The Board of Earth Resource Management"

Confused, Maisy carried the bottle to the kitchen, where Mildred was cheerily making dinner out of freeze-dried moon rations.

"Um, excuse me," Maisy said, taking the bottle and its note to the older woman. "What does this mean? I don't understand."

Mildred turned from her food preparations, and at the sight of the outstretched bottle of wine, her merry demeanor abruptly crumpled into a frown. She shook her head and wiped her hands on a dish towel. "Oh yes. That's from the Resource Board. Their standard offer of compensation. That's what they give all the transplants. I know it really doesn't come close to the worth of your property, but they do their best."

"Wait." It was Maisy's turn to frown. "What do you mean, 'transplants'? What does that have to do with the worth of my property? What property?"

Mildred's eyes widened and her face paled.

"My poor dear, didn't you read the fine print? That contest is part of a new resource management initiative. The Board has taken your Earth-property by now ... you can never go back. Like Alfred and I, you'll be here for the rest of your days."

Author's Note: This one is so short it could probably be called a "flash fiction", but for good reason.

I only had one hour to write it! This story was a result of the Story in a Bag contest held every year at one of our local conventions. Each participant draws 5 random prompts out of 5 different brown bags: a first sentence, a plot, a character, an object, and a location. You have one hour to write a story using ALL 5 prompts in the sci-fi, fantasy, or horror genre (and within a certain page-count limit). This is the story I came up with from my random prompts. I am happy to say this little story won Honorable Mention in the sci-fi category at ConQuesT 45 in 2014, too! (It has, of course, been edited and slightly updated for inclusion in this collection.)

The chronometer in his head clicked.

Fifty-eight.

Fifty-eight days he'd been in this place. In the absolute darkness, the profound silence, counting had kept him sane. He counted the seconds, and the seconds into minutes, the minutes into hours, the hours into days. Sometimes he fell asleep, but the soft click inside his ears would wake him again, and he'd start over.

One, two, three ...

Sometimes they slid a tray of tasteless food under the door, and the metal tray scraped against the rough stone floor fit to make his ears bleed.

They never gave him a fork. Not even a spoon.

He wasn't sure what they expected him to do with any kind of cutlery when his arms were trapped against his body by the straightjacket, but he supposed they didn't want to take any chances.

He'd killed with less.

Shouldn't have gone after her.

He'd known it was a mistake as soon as some no-name orphan on Alpha Station had dropped her name in his lap on a dirty scrap of paper. The Guild had wanted her dead and gone for years now.

They'd attempted to get him to go after her for years now, too. Claimed her betrayal was somehow his fault, somehow related to the unsanctioned relationship he'd had with her. In retrospect, maybe it *was* his fault. He'd initiated the first flirtatious contact. If not for that, maybe there wouldn't have been a relationship at all. No scandalous joining of a Guild member with another Guild member. No heinous crime of falling in love, if that's even what he could have called it.

And no child for the Guild to confiscate at ten years old.

Thus, no reason for her to run.

He sighed heavily into the quiet. They'd tried everything to get him to go after her; bribery, threats, harassment. Until they'd finally resorted to the one thing he couldn't refuse: an official, mandated job. No ANGEL could refuse a job. Not if he wanted to stay alive. And anyway, he had a reputation to uphold.

They'd made her the next name on his list, and Jonathan Septicai never missed a name on his list.

So he'd gone. And now he was here.

Because she'd smelled him coming a kilometer away and he'd stepped right into her trap like some newbie recruit fresh off the street.

So why didn't she just kill you? And why are you still here?

He rolled onto his back on the cold stone floor and stared up into darkness at the invisible ceiling.

She'd warned him about being predictable before, back in the day when they'd been on the same side.

He'd shrugged her off at the time. His targets never knew he was coming, and he'd never needed a second chance at a job. Predictability didn't matter; Jonathan Septicai never missed a mark.

Except Lynn Calipari.

He growled into the blackness.

You're sulking. Stop sulking and get out of here.

"Not sulking," he muttered aloud. "Resting."

Yes, taking a nice holiday seven stories underground in a damp cell that smells of my own shit. Just the vacation I've been dreaming of.

The heavy thump of his cell door unlocking jolted him from the self-pity and he turned his head toward the noise. They hadn't opened that door since the day they'd thrown him in here. Perhaps it was time for an interrogation. Or even more laughable, a trial. The Terran government still had their criminal trials, but they were more staged productions now than real court proceedings. Not that it mattered either way.

Everyone knew the Assassins' National Guild of Extermination and SteaLth existed, but to this day no one had any tangible proof. Even a real trial would have been laughable with such a lack of evidence.

He wriggled his way to a sitting position and squinted in the sudden obtrusion of light as the silhouette of one of the outrageously muscled guards stepped through the doorway. A second guard followed the first, and Jonathon finally rose to his feet to face them, the chain around his ankle clinking with his movement. He winced at the stiffness in his own muscles.

Fifty-eight days. Too long to be off the fitness regimen. Shouldn't have done that. He eyed the two brutes approaching him. Going to make this more difficult.

He let them get close. Let one bend down to unlock the heavy iron cuff around his left ankle.

And just as the man was about to replace the single cuff with a pair of walking ankle cuffs, Jonathan brought his left knee up hard into the man's nose.

He whipped backward and collapsed to the floor, soundless, his face a mass of blood.

Jonathan ducked the second guard's blow and stepped around behind him to kick his legs out from under him. He crashed to the floor alongside his colleague and Jonathan dropped down neatly on top of him, thighs locked around the other man's neck in a second. The guard struggled, trying to twist his body around in an attempt to put Jonathan in a similarly compromising position, but alas, his muscle mass made him far less flexible.

Jonathan closed his eyes and concentrated on keeping an unforgiving pressure on the man's carotid arteries. He counted the seconds, until the second guard's struggles weakened and finally ceased. Jonathan rolled back to his feet. Kept his eyes closed. Shimmied neatly out of the straightjacket ... except for that crotch strap. He reached behind his back and worked patiently at the buckle through the jacket's sleeves, going by feel until it abruptly came loose, dangling free between his legs. Then he pulled the whole contraption up over his head and tossed it like an old shirt.

He grimaced. By the Blades, he *smelled*.

He went to the door and peeked out into the dimly lit corridor. More guards headed his way, apparently having heard the scuffle. He stepped back into his cell's darkness and took a few quick minutes to stretch and limber up before they arrived.

Okay, escape first. Then shower.

It felt good to get a little physical activity again. Get the blood pumping, the adrenaline flowing. He almost wished this wouldn't be so easy.

But then, if they'd really known who he was and what he'd done, they'd never have risked putting him in a cell. They'd have put a bullet in his brain right off, had they really known. No prisons, no interrogations, no trials.

Alas, with no proof of his guild, there was no proof of his deeds. No proof of his list. No one to know how many he'd killed.

No one except Lynn Calipari.

He growled again and set out into the hall as if he

belonged there. Filthy, smelly, sporting an unruly head of hair, a mangy beard, and only half-dressed, Jonathan Septicai ended his so-called vacation.

He eventually reached the visitor's registration lobby and drew up short, taking in the scene of carnage at a glance. No alarms had been tripped, but the prison personnel had all been rendered unconscious in some way or another, temporarily for some, and more permanently for others. His gaze traveled across the many still bodies, eventually reaching the woman who waited for him.

Lynn Calipari.

She granted him a smile, her posture relaxed and casual from where she stood near the registration desk.

But he knew better. She also appeared unarmed, but a lack of weapon had never stood in her way before, and he was quite sure it wouldn't now.

He covered his unease at her appearance with a lopsided grin. "Hello, angel."

She winced at the name. "Don't call me that."

He swept an arm out to encompass the bodies strewn at their feet. "This all for me? A getting-out present? You shouldn't have."

Her smile thinned. "Trust me, it was nothing." A pause, her nose wrinkling. "You look like shit and smell worse. No way in hell you're getting in my car like that."

The impulse to look down at his filthy self was arrested by her last words. "Your car? Wait, you want to give me a ride?

Where? And why? You're the reason I'm here in the first place!"

She shrugged and shook her head, the jet-black hair shifting across her shoulders. So black it shone blue in the light. He used to run his fingers through that shining hair. Used to let her trim, athletic frame curl up next to him, confident she wouldn't put a knife in his back if he rolled over.

He'd stroke her arm as she slept and marvel at the way she could morph from single-minded killer to gentle lover in the space of hours.

He'd never learned how to do that.

But she left the Guild. She's a traitor. She's on your list.

"Because," she said quietly, bringing him back to the present, "I wanted to give you some time ... away. Away from that life, that dogma. I wanted to give you some time alone. To think. I wanted to tell you in person that ... I don't blame you for what happened to our son. The Guild was always going to take him and we were idiots to think otherwise. But ..."

The clear blue eyes hardened and Jonathan tensed, balling his fists. He fought off the memories of their son's Initiation Day ... the day Lynn had run. He didn't think about that day. Didn't think about the kid. Didn't think about her.

"How could you stay with them?" she whispered. "After everything they did to us? After they took him for their brainwashing? After they ordered you to come after *me*?"

He shifted on his feet, hands going to mess at his own greasy locks. "It's ... all I have. All I know. I'm sorry, Lynn."

"Are you?" There was ice in her tone now, her lithe body coiling, and Jonathan braced himself. "You had *me*!" she spat, jabbing at her own chest with a thumb. She took a step forward.

"You had me! You had him!" Another step forward. "Your own son! Your own flesh-and-blood *son*! We weren't enough for you? We didn't matter enough?"

He opened his mouth, but had no words. No words. No excuses. Deep down inside there was still just a void of nothing where there should have been feelings. Guilt? Regret? Shame? He knew they were there somewhere; they came to haunt him in nightmares sometimes, but he just couldn't seem to bring them out when she wanted to see them.

"Tell me right now, Jonathan Septicai," Lynn said through her teeth. "Are you still planning to finish this job?"

He swallowed hard. Flexed his hands and blew out a breath. "I'm sorry," he said again, but she was right. They were mostly just words. Jonathan Septicai never missed a name on his list. Not even for Lynn Calipari, his former lover and mother to his only child.

She nodded slowly, jaw clenching. "Okay," she whispered. "Okay." She drew herself upright, a full six feet of lethal powerhouse. "Goodbye then, Jonathan."

He dropped into a defensive stance, but she just turned and left. He stared after her for a long moment, confused. Then straightened and picked his way over the bodies to the prison's front door.

It had stuck half-ajar, the control panel sparking from Lynn's override handiwork. He slid up to it and pressed his back against it, then risked a quick look out to the front yard.

Lynn had cleared that, too. Automated guard units as well as their human counterparts were motionless, slumped or in pieces. The front gate had been jammed open; it's repetitive, mechanized attempt to close itself was the only sound left in her wake and echoed out across the vast, arid landscape. A prison in the middle of the desert, where the location itself could serve as a deterrent to escape.

He darted across the stretch of dirt and paused again at the gate, searching vainly for any sign of her. She was so damned fast. And so damned good at her job.

No, her ex-job. She's a traitor, remember that.

He'd spent so much time with her all those years ago he'd forgotten how good she was.

So why had she just left like that?

Rows of prison employee cars were parked out front. Lynn had crippled the prison's security system and he had decimated the inside guard force on his way to the lobby, but this quiet wouldn't last forever. Maybe Lynn had revoked her offer of a ride out, but there were plenty here for his choosing. He jogged to the nearest vehicle and jimmied it open, then slipped inside, giving the backseat a cursory look-over. Still no sign of Lynn. Maybe she planned to just keep running.

He shook his head and hit the car's ignition switch, the scrambler chip implanted in his fingertip allowing him instant access. He plotted a suitably inconspicuous route into the navigation system and then engaged it, and the car slid smoothly from its space and out onto the road.

The navigation screen in the dash flickered.

Jonathan tapped at it. The displayed map abruptly disappeared, replaced by a black screen and a crackle of static.

And then Lynn's voice came through the car's speakers, startling him.

"I'm sorry, Jonathan. In your own twisted way I know you must still love me, otherwise you would have tried to kill me just now, in the prison, when I gave you the chance. But I also gave you the chance for an out. And you didn't take that, either. And I can't forgive you for staying with ANGELs after what they did to us. So, I'm sorry. For everything."

He shook his head, exhaling through his teeth. "Lynn, I ..."

"You shouldn't have been so damn predictable."

A countdown splashed up on the screen in brilliant green and the hair on the back of his neck stood up. He fumbled for the door handle.

3, 2, 1 ...

His world exploded into heat and agony.

Burning, everything burning, shrapnel piercing his flesh, the sensation of flying, and for one, brief moment ... true, painful regret.

Author's Note: *Another prompt, another story.*

This short came about as part of a challenge at The Writer's Arena (http://www.thewritersarena.com). I asked to be allowed to participate, and the keepers of the arena graciously obliged. Our prompt was "prison break". Myself and one other author had one week to write a story relating to this prompt. Our stories were then posted on their website and judged: readers voted for which story was their favorite, and then the 3 arena judges gave their opinion. The story with the most combined total votes was declared the winner of that week's challenge. Happily, A.N.G.E.L.s was declared the winner! Funny enough, the characters Jonathan and Lynn from this tale also star in that space opera thriller Guardian Angel mentioned previously (and in fact, Gray is part of Jonathan's backstory. This story could be considered an "alternate reality" for him, I suppose)...

PUPPET

I thought I was invisible. I was wrong.

The creatures of this alien planet took notice of me as soon as I stepped out of the pod. They were hulking, six-legged beasts, with translucent skin and long, waving antennae ... and large, sharp teeth I calculated with 54% certainty would penetrate the graphite fibers of my outer casing.

I froze as they lifted their heads and sniffed the dense, muggy air of this planet. They had no eyes, but their antennae leaned in my direction, their lips drawing back in soundless snarls. My self-preservation protocol activated, urging my treads to reverse and scramble back inside the pod to safety. But mission directives stopped me.

Dr. Adrastea Summers had been certain in her decision to send me instead of a human astronaut.

I could do what humans could not, she'd told the Board. I could set foot on this planet without the need for complex gear or habitats, thus saving the tax-payers billions of dollars. With the ever-rising costs of plague containment, her proposal had met little resistance. As a Privatized Utilitarian Patrol and Preparation of Environment Tank, I would not question my purpose as a human might on this mission. Nor would I be tempted to sabotage it in pursuit of selfish gains. I would not draw the attention of the local fauna, either, especially with Dr. Summers' patented light-bending cells installed across my surface. They were supposed to make me, in effect, invisible.

On that part at least, she had been entirely incorrect.

But I did not want to disappoint her. While the United Coalition of Governments had sent me here to save the human race, Dr. Summers had sent me here for something far more important: to save the galaxy.

She hadn't told the Board that part. But I'd heard her whispering to her assistant, and the subroutines buried deep in my primary directives were clear.

I could not fail.

The nearest beast took a step toward me, its antennae dipping and rising like living things themselves. My processors whirred fiercely in my chassis, mission directives warring with my self-preservation protocol. I couldn't very well succeed if shredded to pieces, could I?

Saliva dripped from its gaping maw, and I checked and re-checked the functionality of the "invisibility" light cells. My diagnosis insisted they were fully operational. This was the flaw, then, in planning a mission without sufficient knowledge of the terrain or its lifeforms. My data on this planet was slim. Most interstellar travelers avoided this place. And after seeing these creatures close up, I understood why. But a very important ship had crashed here. The ship carrying the Final Element; the object the UCG believed held the cure to the terrible disease that had befallen humanity at First Contact.

The Volans had come in peace. Only days later, humanity had been decimated with a plague like none ever seen in the history of its evolution.

Most of planet Earth blamed the Volans, of course.

But the leaders of the UCG, including Dr. Summers, knew the truth. The Volans were to be the saviors of humanity, not the destroyers of it.

That crashed Volan ship ... that wreckage was my goal. Only four of the six-legged animals stood between me and it.

And within it, the cargo. The Final Element.

They called it a patchwork quilt, for lack of a better translation. An alien quilt, constructed of living threads and used to heal any bodily injury, any kind of sickness. It was the cure to save all of humanity.

Or, as Dr. Summers had often discussed with her assistant, it would be what destroyed all of humanity. The value of such a thing could not be measured. Who could be trusted with such a priceless item?

I could; that was my purpose. The hydraulics attached to my treads activated, lifting me a little higher. If I'd been able to make the sound, I would have laughed. A P.U.P.P.E.T. on a hostile planet, risking its own self-awareness for a patchwork quilt. It sounded even more absurd than the conspiracy theorists who claimed the Volans had poisoned the humans on purpose.

Of course that wasn't true.

Directives finally aligned in my processors and I sprinted forward abruptly, dodging between two of the massive beasts before they could turn.

I sped toward the wreckage, my flexible treads bouncing over deep red rocks and fluorescent blue plants. Thunderous galloping followed close behind, and one of the animals let out a horrific shriek. I dove through a hole in the wrecked ship's side and the beasts slammed into the hull, too big to come through. I skidded away from their searching claws, then made my way to the cargo hold.

I heard them snuffling and growling behind me, the noises reverberating in the crumpled ship's interior. Their claws screeched against the metal as they tore away chunks of hull. They would get through soon enough. I didn't have much time.

But the Final Element was easy to find. It was the only thing in the cavernous cargo bay, and it shone like a beacon from within its clear transport capsule. The living threads pulsed with a warm, golden energy. I extended my arms and entered the code given to the UCG by the Volan High Command. The capsule popped open with a hiss, stirring up a cloud of fine red dust. I reached inside and picked up the quilt with the five-fingered hands Dr. Summers had designed for me. I marveled at it. So beautiful. So perfect. So clean. And so alien.

Beings that had created something this magnificent and given it out freely, with no return demands, could never have designed the plague that now ravaged Earth. My logic centers knew this, and so did Dr. Summers. The Volans had not poisoned Earth; human extremists had done it themselves in their suspicion and paranoia, through clumsy efforts to undermine the First Contact peace talks. Their short-sighted actions had backfired, as they usually did, and the bio-weapon they'd hoped would put an end to the Volans had instead brought disaster to their own species.

Dr. Summers was tired of the suspicion, the distrust, and the terracentric xenophobes. Tired of the paranoia, the sabotage, the war-mongering, the plague. And so was I.

A great crash echoed down the corridor, followed by the squeal of rending metal. The monsters had broken through the smashed hull; my heat sensors relayed a proximity warning even as I felt the tremble of their footsteps through my treads. Their panting breaths echoed in the dark, closer and closer. By my best estimates, they would reach me in sixty seconds. My subroutines initiated, urgent and precise: a lowly P.U.P.P.E.T. was to save the galaxy.

I had the Final Element, the Cure, the one living quilt

engineered to the genetic code of Homo sapiens. The quilt that could save all of humanity.

There could and would be no duplicate. I held it up in triumph.

Then, I carried out mission directive Priority One. I took the action that would ultimately cleanse the galaxy of the greatest plague yet known to the universe:

I destroyed it.

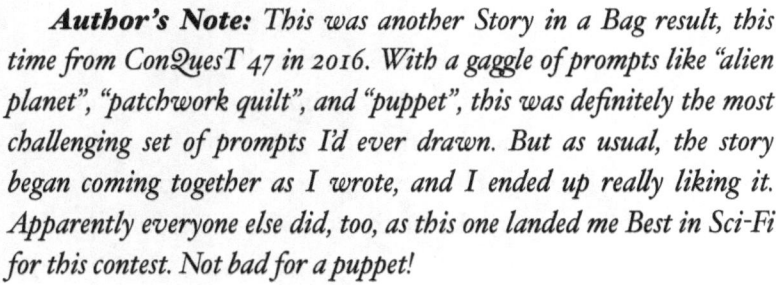

Author's Note: *This was another Story in a Bag result, this time from ConQuesT 47 in 2016. With a gaggle of prompts like "alien planet", "patchwork quilt", and "puppet", this was definitely the most challenging set of prompts I'd ever drawn. But as usual, the story began coming together as I wrote, and I ended up really liking it. Apparently everyone else did, too, as this one landed me Best in Sci-Fi for this contest. Not bad for a puppet!*

A LOVELY DAY FOR A PARADE

He watched the ship as it hovered, then landed no more than five feet in front of him. Hot air blasted over him on a wave of dust, and he threw an arm over his nose and mouth, coughing. The ship's engines powered down with a heavy whine, the access ramp hissing as it opened. Zakary glanced over his shoulder, back to the noise of the parade still clanging and banging down Main Street. They had agents there too, he knew, but he might have a chance of getting lost in the crowd...

He turned and bolted back down the alleyway.

Boots hit the ground behind him. Soon after came an echoing shout, and the sizzling blue blast of an ionic stunner shot over his shoulder. He increased speed, pumped his arms, and crashed into the ranks of the local high school band full force.

Clarinets and tubas went flying. A few spectators screamed as another ionic blast zapped the nearest drummer and dropped him to the pavement in a heap.

"Sorry, sorry," Zakary mumbled, then shoved away from a shocked flutist and tore off through the forward ranks of the parade. If he could get to the werewolf float, maybe he could duck inside.

They always had the largest displays, and besides, Gregor owed him a favor for getting that distemper vaccine.

More screams and even more curses followed in his wake as he dodged color guards and baton throwers, clowns and antique cars and a fire department hovercraft. He saw the werewolf float ahead, so close, but then the roar of the

Marshal's ship thundered overhead and he instinctively ducked, almost falling flat on his face. The ship circled above the parade, which now more closely resembled a disorganized riot as people panicked and ran.

Gregor himself rode atop the werewolves' float, a giant round moon advertising their newest werewolf-friendly brew, supposedly meant to ease the transition from human to wolf to human again. Everything was easier with a little alcohol, wasn't it?

Well, that's what they say, anyway. Zakary leapt onto the base of the float, clinging to the side of the moon. "Gregor!"

The werewolf stared up at the ship, awash in the swirling dust, but at the sound of his name he turned, and Zakary almost lost his grip on the papier-mâché as the man gave him a ferocious snarl.

"You brought them *here*? How dare you!"

Zakary frowned, surprised at his friend's ire.

"I didn't mean to—"

The ship opened fire and obliterated the false moon in a fantastic shower of flames. Zakary briefly flew, the world reduced to a swirling mass of burning strips of colored paper. White flashed across his vision as he landed hard and rolled, then moaned in the dirt. Acrid smoke stung his nose.

Pain dug into his ribs. All he could see now were fleeing feet and tiny fires still burning on the debris. Howling joined the screams, long low howls and keening high howls, and the hairs on his arms stood up. He knew what that meant.

He pushed himself to his feet and dared to glance back to where his friend once stood.

There were only bodies, surrounded by the remaining survivors of the pack, all howling their mourning song.

A third blast from a stunner skimmed past Zakary's nose

so close he smelled ozone, jolting him out of his daze. He swore and turned to run again just as the other werewolves twisted to glare at him. They tore off after him and he knew his plan to hide in the parade had been a truly terrible idea.

He ran through alleyways and back streets, now chased by the Marshal from the ship as well as a pack of furious werewolves, and his hopes of escape dwindled as quickly as his breath.

He brought up his comm and hit the speed dial. "Lily! I need pick up right now!"

"Who did you piss off this time?" she drawled back, unconcerned, as if they were on vacation.

"They found me, damnit! The Marshal found me! Get down here right now!"

"Why didn't you say so?" She clicked off the line and Zakary swore again, lungs and legs burning. Sweat plastered his shirt to his skin and ran into his eyes; the dust choked him. The pounding feet behind were gaining, gaining ... were-wolves were ridiculously fast; they would be on him soon, and changed or not they would rip out his throat...

A colorful blob appeared out of the side alley in front of him and a driving force stopped Zakary in his tracks as efficiently as a brick wall, throwing him backward to land heavily on his back.

His teeth jarred together and he lay still, aching every-where, gasping for air, heart throbbing in his temples.

One of the clowns from the parade leered over him, his overly large painted smile truly evil. "Thought you could escape, eh? Not this time, boy."

But then the werewolves were on them.

"Back off, clowny," one of them panted. "This is our fresh meat."

"I think not," a female voice replied, and Zakary looked up in a daze to see a woman in a leather corset approach, her knee-high black boots brown with dust, a Marshal's badge on her shoulder. "We've been after this one for a long time. No way you curs are taking him from us."

"Do all Marshals wear corsets?" Zakary coughed, then wished he wouldn't have opened his mouth.

She pointed the stunner at him, right at his nose, but one of the werewolves stepped in front of it.

"I told you, he's ours," the man growled.

The sound of thrusters washed them all in vibration, and then a very familiar personal transport vehicle hovered overhead, its small but effective cannons trained on the crowd of people clustered around Zakary's prone form.

He grinned despite himself. "Lily," he gasped, "your timing is impeccable."

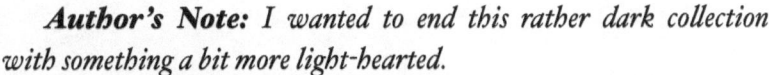

Author's Note: I wanted to end this rather dark collection with something a bit more light-hearted.

This short was yet another Story in a Bag result, from all the way back in 2013. This was my very first venture into the Story in a Bag challenge, and to my utmost surprise, won Best in Sci-Fi my very first year! I was thrilled. Yes, I know, I wouldn't expect werewolves in my sci-fi either, but what was I supposed to do with that first line and a plot prompt of "being chased by a pack of angry werewolves"? As you can see, my hands were tied. But there's the idea out there that the more limitations you are given in something, the more creative you become in order to work within those limitations and still make things work. Similar to that well-known adage, "Necessity is the mother of invention." If there is anything these Story in a Bag adventures and other prompt-based stories have taught me, it's that this is very, very true! So I hope you enjoyed this last little genre mix-up ... and like many of these shorts, this one has also spawned its very own novel, working title of Hound of God , coming soon! But for now, this is...

END OF LINE

MANY THANKS TO MY LAUNCH TEAM!

I couldn't have done it without you: Zaneta, Sandy, Pat, Aura, Caitlin, Vicky, Tiffiney, Donald, and Rob; and my patrons Pat, Vicky, Ian, and Kristin!

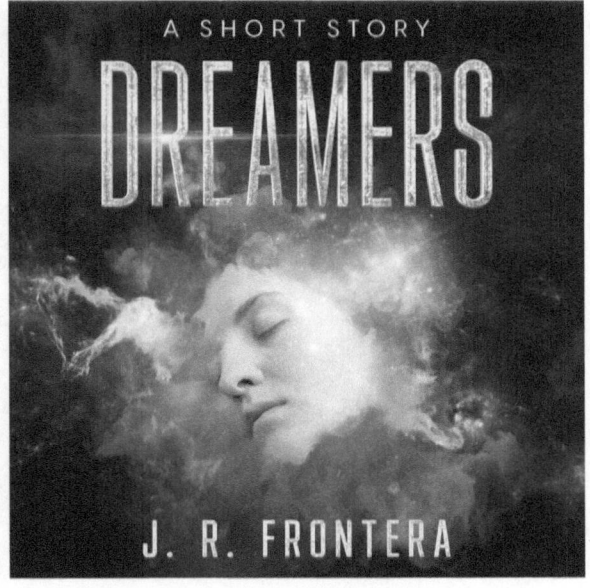

ABOUT THE AUTHOR

J. R. Frontera has been telling stories in some form or another since she could hold a crayon and draw. Her love of science fiction and fantasy originated with her early exposure to the worlds of *Star Wars*, *Star Trek*, *Lord of the Rings*, and *Dune*. Exploring the potential and pitfalls of humanity in future or fantastical worlds is a temptation she's just never been able to resist. She loves to write rebel stories for rebel souls, and co-founded a local writing group known as The Wordwraiths. She's also co-owner of their publishing imprint Wordwraith Books. When she's not writing, momming, or working at her full-time job, she's often horseback riding, playing videogames, or cosplaying. She lives in rural Missouri with her husband, son, and more animals than she'd prefer to disclose. You can find out more about J. R. Frontera and her books by visiting her website at https:// jrfrontera.com.

www.ingramcontent.com/pod-product-compliance
Lightning Source LLC
Chambersburg PA
CBHW032112170626
46808CB00008B/3030